DAVID'S DRAWINGS

DAVID'S DRAWINGS

Story and Pictures
by
Cathryn Falwell

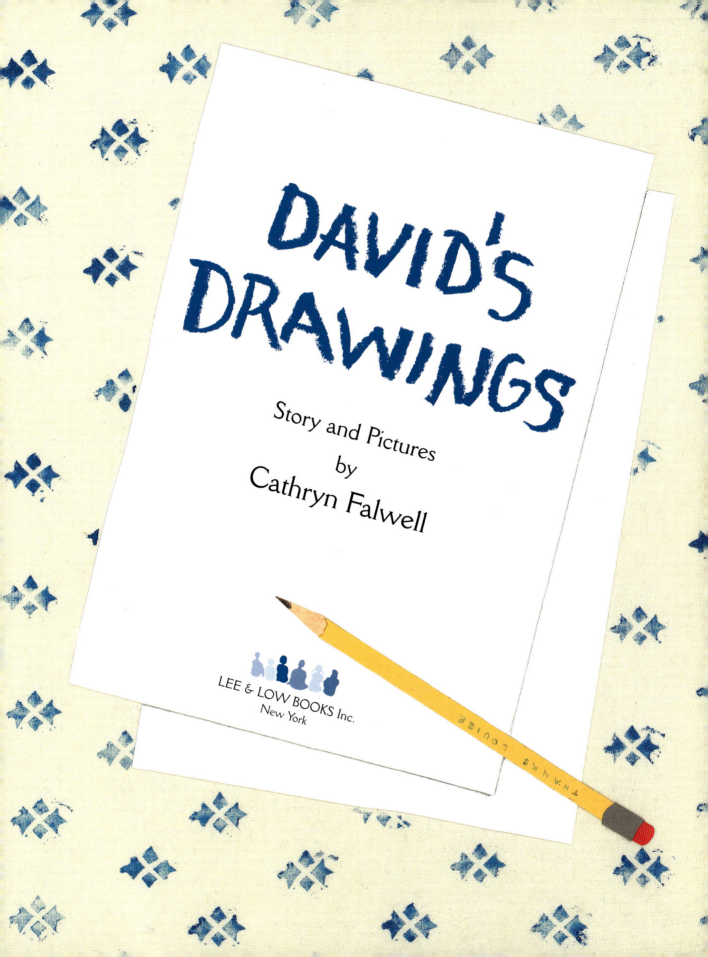

LEE & LOW BOOKS Inc.
New York

*F*or teachers and parents
who help to nurture the
creative spirit of children
—*C.F.*

Manufactured in China by South China Printing Co.,
May 2011

Book design by David Neuhaus/NeuStudio
Book production by The Kids at Our House

The text is set in 18-point Della Robbia
The illustrations are rendered in cut paper and fabric collage

HC 10 9 8 7 6
PB 10 9 8 7
First Edition

Library of Congress Cataloging-in-Publication Data
Falwell, Cathryn.
David's drawings / by Cathryn Falwell.— 1st ed.
p. cm.
Summary: A shy African American boy arriving at a new school
makes friends with his classmates by drawing a picture of a tree.
ISBN 978-1-58430-031-1 (hc)   ISBN 978-1-58430-261-2 (pbk)
[1. First day of school—Fiction. 2. Schools—Fiction.
3. Drawing—Fiction. 4. Friendship—Fiction. 5. African
Americans—Fiction.] I. Title.
PZ7.F198 Dav 2001   [E]—dc21   2001016450

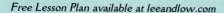

Free Lesson Plan available at leeandlow.com

Irvin L. Young Memorial Library
Whitewater, Wisconsin

One gray winter day,
David saw a beautiful tree.

When he got to school,
David took off his boots
and hung up his jacket.
He found a pencil and
a fresh piece of paper.

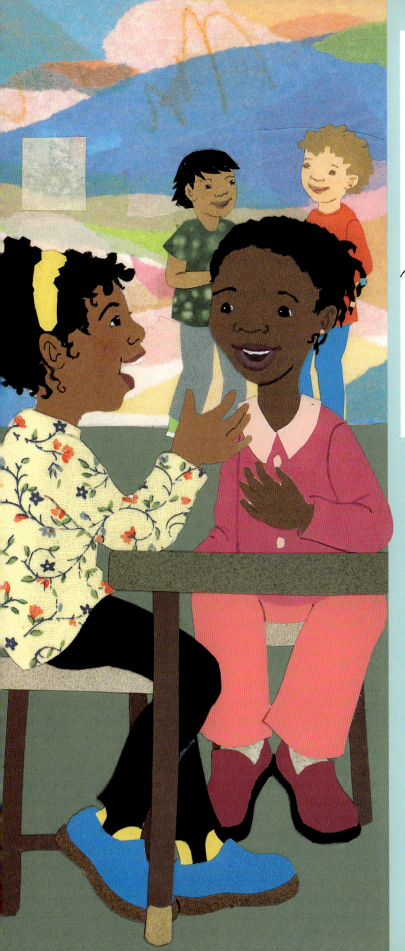

David thought for a moment.
Then he made a drawing
of the tree he had seen.

"Nice tree," said Amanda.
"But it needs color."
David got some crayons
and made the tree brown.

Amanda smiled.
"Some grass, too," she said.
David handed her
a green crayon.
"Here. You can make some,"
he said shyly.
Amanda colored green grass
under the tree.

"That tree needs leaves,"
Ryan said.
David looked at his
drawing and then began
to add leaves.
He let Ryan add a few more.

"Look!" said Jamal. "I have
these cool stickers. May I
put some on the picture?"
"Sure," said David.

"I know. It needs a person—
like me!" Laurel said.
She grinned and drew a girl.

"It needs a boy, too,"
said Carlos.
"Okay," said David.
Carlos drew a boy
with an orange shirt.

Kira quickly added
a row of fluffy clouds.
Brandon drew a cat
and a dog.
Thea added a smiling turtle.

"Birds would look nice,"
said Lee May. She drew
two flying in the sky.

"It needs a rainbow, too!"
said Rosie. She set to work
with a fistful of colors.

The bell rang for class
to begin.
"That was fun," said Ryan.
"We made a great picture,"
said Kira.
"See you at recess, David?"
asked Amanda.
"Sure!" David agreed.

Nick

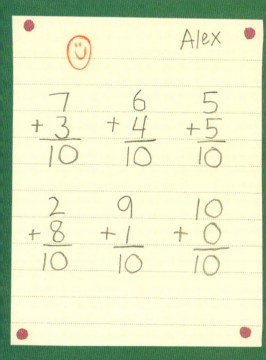

Alex

$$\begin{array}{r} 7 \\ +\ 3 \\ \hline 10 \end{array} \qquad \begin{array}{r} 6 \\ +\ 4 \\ \hline 10 \end{array} \qquad \begin{array}{r} 5 \\ +\ 5 \\ \hline 10 \end{array}$$

$$\begin{array}{r} 2 \\ +\ 8 \\ \hline 10 \end{array} \qquad \begin{array}{r} 9 \\ +\ 1 \\ \hline 10 \end{array} \qquad \begin{array}{r} 10 \\ +\ 0 \\ \hline 10 \end{array}$$

Our Class Picture.

At the end of the day, David looked at the picture again. Then he wrote Our Class Picture neatly on the bottom and hung it on the bulletin board.

David walked home from school.
On the way, he saw the beautiful tree.

When he got home,
David took off his boots
and hung up his jacket.
He found a pencil and
a fresh piece of paper.

David thought for a moment.
Then he made a drawing
of the tree he had seen.

David's sister came over
to the table.
"Nice drawing," she said.
"But it needs something."

David looked up.
His sister smiled.
"It needs . . .

My Drawing.

. . . to hang on your wall!"

"I think so, too," said David.
Then he wrote
My Drawing
neatly on the bottom
and hung the picture
right above his bed.